SILVER BELLS

A Holiday Romance Novella by Jacquie Biggar

Silver Bells

By Jacquie Biggar

Dedication

For my Family,

Without them, I am nothing.

Also, I want to dedicate this story to the winner of our Fresh Fiction contest, Debra Philippon, who chose Silver Bells as her favorite Christmas song.

This is what she said:

I was quite thrilled to hear I had won a dedication, and

Silver Bells has always been my favorite (secular) Christmas song. My mother loved it, too, and

always hummed it when she was doing the Christmas baking and decorating. She couldn't sing

for beans, something I inherited from her, so she always hummed it :-)

Deb

What Readers Are Saying

The Guardian

The opening of this story is so gripping and heartbreaking that I couldn't stop reading. I had to find out what happened to Lucas, Scott and Natalya...and to Tracy, a Medical Examiner whose comfortable but bland workaholic life is never the same after fate brings a couple of super-famous movie stars to her morgue. Soon her life and her heart are in danger and so is everyone around her. Love the mix of paranormal and contemporary worlds where humans and angels, heroes and villains, friends and lovers collide in a quest for love and forgiveness.

J. Read

Ms Biggar has made a big splash here with her first paranormal romance. The book hooked me from the very start. Add some twists, turns, suspense and romance and you get one great read.

Barbara

The Sheriff Meets His Match

Ya just gotta love Jack.... Jack is the sexy sheriff in the town of Tidal Falls who has dedicated his life to his job and raising his daughter. You see, Jack's ex-wife took off and left him not only a broken man but a single man with a child to raise on his own. Needless to say Jack has closed off his heart to longterm relationships.

But when a sassy, totally disorganized yet gorgeous women, Laurel, comes to town and is given a temp job at the Sheriff's office, it test's Jack's ability to not only resist her but to stay sane. Needless to say these two push all the wrong buttons while trying to fight an attraction neither wants to admit, especially when her uncle comes to town. (Laurel's uncle is a professional con-man and often running from the law). And once again, he brings trouble to Laurel's door.

This is a funny, lighthearted romance that will keep you laughing at this crazy bunch while guessing what in the world is going to happen next.

A Huge WTG to Ms. Biggar for this delightful tale in the Lonely Hearts series.

By Barbara Barber

CHAPTER ONE

Christy Taylor smiled at the teens performing
skateboard tricks on a set of iron rails, the screech-
scrape of their wheels a musical accompaniment to
the slap-slap of her sneakers hitting the pavement as
she jogged past. Though it was early December on
Vancouver Island the sun sat like a warm treat on her
shoulders. Snowberries lined the pathway on the
Goose Walking Trail, crunching beneath her feet. The
unparalleled beauty of the Pacific Ocean lay off to her
right. A salty breeze carried the scents of wood, brine,
and soil to clear the fog from her brain. The past
couple of years had been tough. Between Jill's illness

and the increasing costs in rent it was a never-ending battle to keep everything afloat.

She followed the snaky course through Beacon Hill Park, dodging dogs and children and couples holding hands. At the boat pond a father patiently taught his young son how to run the remote control for a jaunty red sailboat, while Mallard ducks paddled nearby searching for scraps.

She turned left and took the path that led her to the seawall, her favorite part of the run.

And there he was.

Every time she'd come by here for the past two months the same man crouched on the furthest edge of the breakwater, staring out to sea.

He captivated her.

She'd sit on the little spit of sand several feet away and create stories in her head about him. Maybe he was a Russian prince cast out of his homeland. Or a spy waiting on a boat bringing him information meant to save the world. Or maybe even a merman cast upon the shore and unable to find his way back to his watery home. The last brought a wry smile to her lips. Her mom always said she had a writer's imagination.

She opened her fanny pack and drew out a bottle of water, a strip of homemade peach fruit leather, and her drawing supplies. She loved capturing nature on paper with nothing more than a few graphite pencils in varying grades and Caran d'Ache Luminance colors for shading. Her art was slowly gaining recognition, though it was taking more time than she could afford.

Sunset gradually lightened the horizon from chilly winter's grey-blue to neon orange, brilliant fuchsia, and canary yellow. Nimble fingers flew over the page, eager to catch every nuance as it occurred. Her unsuspecting model never moved, his silhouette perfectly captured by the dying rays of the sun.

When it became too dark to draw, Christy set the pad aside and twisted the cap off her water bottle. The liquid was a benediction going down her parched throat. She drank most of it before replacing the lid with a satisfied sigh. The day hadn't begun well, but at least it was ending on a high note. She felt good about the work she'd just produced. It would be easier to tell after she returned to the shop and finished the shading of course, but she was off to a decent start.

Shivering a little now the sun had gone down, she returned everything to the bag and zipped it closed, then stood and brushed the sand from her butt and thighs before bending to pick up the fanny pack. Time to head home, her daughter would be waiting.

A pair of dark brown hiking boots—size enormous—came into her line of sight. Her heart skipped a beat. Most people on the island were friendly, but she *was* a woman on her own, and it was rapidly becoming dark. How stupid.

She tightened her grip on the bag and cursing the fact she'd been so irresponsible, slowly rose to her feet, her gaze following the long, clean line of jean-clad legs, dark cotton shirt, tucked in and belted at the waist, open leather jacket, and chiseled jawline covered in a day's worth of stubble. Glittering eyes stared at her from a deeply tanned, aloof-looking face.

"Quit following me." The voice matched his visage, cold, harsh, and unforgiving.

So much for her fantasy hero. Christy stiffened and glared. "Kind of full of yourself, aren't you?"

He leaned back and crossed his arms, his stance unforgiving. And to think she'd found him intriguing. Ha, more like infuriating.

"So it's just a coincidence every time I turn around, there you are?" He lifted a hand and rubbed the back of his neck. The rasping sound along with the backdrop of the swishing waves made her— restless.

"Look, I don't do interviews, okay? Not even for cute little pixies. Tell your boss, next time I'll call the cops."

Incredulity overrode her apprehension. "Are you serious? I have as much right to be on this beach as you do, buddy. Trust me, you're not half as fascinating as you seem to think you are."

In between one breath and the next, Mr. Personality seized the bag out of her grip and delved inside.

"Hey, give that back," she cried, trying to wrestle it out of his grasp.

"If you have nothing to hide…" He pulled the drawings free and turned his wall of a back on her.

Christy couldn't believe this was happening. Adrenaline zipped through her body, leaving her feeling more alive than she had in a long while. And it was all due to this… this jerk ripping pages out of her workbook while she stood by helpless to do anything about it. All that work—gone.

"Please," she begged, her throat husky. "I meant no harm. I draw for a living. That's all they are, drawings."

At least the shredding stopped.

He leveled his gaze on her again, as though deciding whether to throw the whole bag out to sea or not. She really hoped not. It had taken months to save for those pencils. They were the very best and made a huge difference to the level of her workmanship.

"Please," she said again.

He hesitated, then folded the sheets of paper he'd taken and shoved them into his jacket pocket before handing over her bag.

"Next time you might try asking," he said dryly.

As he clumped away in those heavy boots his voice floated back to her on the breeze. "The answer would've been no, by the way."

Was it too much to ask that he trip over his enormous—arrogance?

CHAPTER TWO

Christy opened the door painted a cheerful robin's-egg blue at the back of the Wandering Mind Studio and smiled, relieved to hear her young daughter's laughter. She hadn't meant to be gone so long, but it seemed like Jill was fine.

"Where's my girl?" she called, setting her backpack on the counter.

"Mommy, Mommy," Jill cried, skipping into the kitchen. "Guess what? We've been playing *I Spy*. It's so fun, and I was winning too." She came and wrapped her arms around Christy's waist. "I'm hungry," she announced.

Christy bent over and kissed the top of Jill's head, then smiled at the elderly woman entering the room. "Was she good?"

Claire Michaels, her neighbor and good friend, snorted. "Do geese lay eggs?" she asked, and grinned at Jill's giggles. "Of course she was good. That child is never a problem. How about you? Did you enjoy your run?"

Annoyance warmed her cheeks to a rosy hue. "I did until some idiot took offence to me drawing him and stole my work."

Claire gasped. "Phone the police. He can't get away with that."

Christy grimaced. "He kind of can. I should have asked his permission first. I've just never had an issue before." She shrugged and let go of Jill so she could open the fridge to withdraw the soup she'd made earlier.

"Want to stay for dinner? There's plenty." She waved a hand back and forth over the tricky gas burner until it lit, then set the pot of hamburger soup on to heat.

"Stay, Aunty Claire. Stay," Jill begged.

Claire laughed. "How can I say no to an invitation like that?" She sat at the oval country style kitchen table with a relieved sigh and watched Jill dance around the island in the center of the room. "She never stops. It's hard to imagine…"

Christy's stomach rolled. She nodded and concentrated on cutting slices of fresh baked whole wheat bread to go with the meal. Yeah, it *was* hard to imagine her bright, cheerful little girl had developed the dangerous disease of Type 1 Diabetes. But it was true.

The shock had taken a while to overcome. To think a simple trip to the clinic over a weak set of kidneys ended in emergency at the hospital. Then came a week spent in the children's ward learning just how threatening her sickness could be—and that there is no cure. It was a lot to take in and deal with. It broke her heart every time she had to poke her daughter's fingers in order to take blood glucose readings, twelve or more times a day, twenty-four-seven. And then there were the needles for insulin injections. Some days it was hard to remember a life before carb counts and two-hour checks, but the worst were the nights. The fear was always there she'd be fast asleep and Jill would go low and need immediate care, or dangerously high requiring ketone checks and lots and lots of water to flush her system.

The stress had ended her marriage. Kevin was a good man, but not up to dealing with his less than perfect—in his eyes—little girl. And that was okay, Christy didn't have the reserves to deal with his crisis of conscience anyway.

She gave the bubbling, fragrant soup a stir and carried the bread plate to the table. "Claire, can you make us a cup of tea while I get Jill ready?"

Claire patted her hand with bony, arthritic fingers. "Of course. Take your time, honey. I'll watch the soup."

Christy nodded her gratitude and turned to Jill who was playing with her doll on the floor near the water cooler. "C'mon, sweetheart. Let's go get washed before dinner."

By the time they returned, Claire had ladled the soup and set the table. Jill ran over and scrambled into her booster seat and Christy handed her a slice of bread. Once they were settled, she lifted her cup and inhaled the flowery bergamot tea. There was something about a good cup of tea that washed away even the most stressful days. Or at least made them easier to bear.

"So tell me about your model. Was he hot?" Claire asked, her faded blue eyes twinkling.

Christy gasped and swallowed her tea wrong. She started coughing and choking and had to wipe her teary eyes on a napkin before she could speak. "He's not *my* model. I'm pretty sure he was thinking of throwing me into the ocean along with my work."

"You went swimming, Mommy?" Little Miss Big Ears asked.

Christy grimaced and pushed her daughter's bowl a little closer. "No, I did not go swimming. Now quit eavesdropping and eat your dinner. You already had your insulin, you can't play around, honey."

Jill pouted for a moment, her lower lip jutting out far enough to catch a fly, then she picked up her spoon and dug into her meal like a real trooper. Christy hated coming off heavy-handed, but there was no choice. Her daughter's days of dawdling at the dinner table were over.

"Joel stopped by while you were gone," Claire said, her gaze sympathetic.

Great. What did her landlord want this time? She'd yet to meet the man, but his cryptic phone calls via a harried sounding secretary didn't bode well.

"Did he leave a message?"

"Just said he'd try and catch you tomorrow." Claire stretched over and swiped Jill's chin. "I think you'd like him."

Claire kept trying to put her matchmaking skills to work, and that was a problem. Christy didn't have time for a relationship. And even if she did, it wouldn't be with the man who held her fate in his hands.

CHAPTER THREE

Joel Carpenter rubbed the back of his neck in the futile hope of easing some of the strain, and stared out the plate-glass window at the Gorge Waterway. In the months since renting the house overlooking the estuary, he'd spent hours upon hours looking outside and hoping the brick wall he'd built in his mind would crumble and set him free. He had both his agent and his editor breathing down his neck, but still couldn't get the words to magically appear on his computer screen.

In fourteen bestselling books this had never happened to him before. Maybe his career as a fictional crime-fighter was over.

Great, now even his thoughts were getting lame.

Frustrated, he slammed the lid down on his laptop and rose to wander through the old Victorian home. He'd rented it hoping to immerse himself in his hero's latest case, *The Lady Said No*, but so far the lady wasn't talking and Augustus had no case. Gus was the much-loved detective who somehow bumbled his way through every situation Joel threw his way.

Until now.

His shoes squeaked on the uneven grooving of the hardwood flooring. The stained glass window in the front entry let rays of multi-hued light into the hall and decorated the walls with a rainbow of color. The heavy oak used on the door was copied in the construction of the handrail leading to the second floor. The staircase was wide and sweeping, perfect for a murder scene, if only his heroine would cooperate.

The problem was he'd become attached to her. She had spunk, something Joel couldn't bring himself to dim the light on, and yet she was perfect for the role of victim. Scandalous in the story's early nineteen hundred's time period, she was an unwed mother who owned her own seamstress business. All admirable qualities, but it was the rebellion shining from her fascinating green eyes, and the sarcasm that fell from those luscious red lips, that made it impossible for Joel to end her life.

She was taking over his story and he didn't like it.

He continued his tour down a long hallway decorated with dark wainscoting and ended in his favorite room; a solarium poised so far over the bank of the inlet it felt as though he were on the water. It was filled with green plants, the air redolent of moist soil, perfume from a flowering Magnolia bush, and brine from the salt waters beyond the wall of windows cracked open to let the fresh breeze flow throughout the room.

Victoria was similar to his home in Scotland. He could see what had drawn his grandmother to stay. She'd taken a cruise as a young woman, met her Canadian husband, and never returned. He didn't blame her. If he could evade his family he would too.

She'd looked good when he'd seen her last night. Better than he remembered as a child. He wasn't so sure about the property he'd bought as an investment, however. It needed repairs, and the tenant seemed to have an issue with paying the rent on time. To complicate matters, apparently his grandmother had become friends with the woman and urged him to be more lenient.

He didn't have time to chase after someone who didn't know how to handle responsibility. His father had ground that particular trait into his brain.

Restless, Joel paced the boundaries of the room like a caged animal. He'd promised himself he wouldn't leave the house until he nailed the next chapter down, but the way he was going it wouldn't be before Christmas. And to make matters worse, the manuscript was due January first. He'd never even come close to blowing a deadline before, and the pressure was getting to him. If only the lady of the manor would do what he wanted, the rest of the book would fall into place. All he had to do was convince her to face her fate.

Chilled but reluctant to close out the fresh air, Joel reached for his jacket, and frowned at the crinkling sound coming from the pocket. He had scraps of paper with notes jotted on every surface lying all over the house, but didn't remember shoving anything into his coat. The crumpled mess revealed a drawing of the ocean, complete with ragged, jutting rocks and the figure of a man highlighted in the setting sun. His figure.

The woman had done a commendable job portraying the strength and solitude of the scene. If only she hadn't included him in the picture. And, yeah, okay, he might be acting paranoid—after all, it was only his back as he crouched looking out at the water—but dammit, he worked hard for his privacy. If she were one of the myriad reporters that dogged his every step, he'd sue whatever publication she worked for so fast their heads would spin.

Since his rise to literary stardom, Joel had seen it all. From women who fabricated ways to meet him so they could exploit the relationship, to men he'd thought were his friends sell off pieces of his life like so much confetti. He was done with it. Stick to himself and no one could hurt him again, including the grandmother he hadn't seen since a child. He was determined to maintain a safe distance. He'd drop in once in a while to make sure she was doing all right, it would have to be enough.

He couldn't believe she'd tried to set him up with the flighty tenant living next door. It was bad enough he had to have his PA chase after her for the rent, he didn't need his grandmother making fake excuses so they could meet. She swore she hadn't revealed his secret, but he couldn't bring himself to trust her, or anyone else for that matter. There was a price to pay for fame. Sometimes he regretted that first book. It had rocketed his career, and nothing had been the same since.

He gazed at the picture he'd been unconsciously straightening and wondered about the woman who had made the drawing. His lips quirked remembering her feistiness after he'd given her his warning. She'd surprised him. Most backed away when faced with his well-known temper. Not her. She'd given as good as she got. Her animated face in the evening shadows had fascinated him. Her trim, athletic body attracted him instantly.

Dangerously.

Joel had been down that road before, and was still paying the price. He wouldn't let it happen again.

CHAPTER FOUR

Christy stretched one of her prints over a smart-looking blue steel frame and snapped the back edge into place. She'd just propped it up and stepped back to get a look when a group of Asian tourists strolled into *The Wandering Mind Studio.* Business at the little boutique store had been brisk the past few weeks thanks to the depressed Canadian dollar. Victoria was a popular holiday destination and many artisans had flocked to the region to reap the benefits. Her included.

After the disintegration of her marriage to Kevin, she'd made the tough decision to leave everyone she knew and move to the coast. It hadn't been easy, but she didn't regret her choice. Kevin was a well-known and well-respected lawyer in their hometown. It was too hard to move on with her life when everyone kept asking if they were going to work their problems out. They weren't. His betrayal when she'd needed him the most, had cut too deep, it wasn't something she could easily set aside. Any guilt she had about taking Jill so far away from her father was superseded by his lack of interest in her welfare. How could a man who came from a large family and had many nephews and nieces be so cold to his own daughter?

She smiled at the elderly lady admiring the drawing she'd done of Jill, pail in hand, searching for shells on a windswept beach. Flocks of ducks and geese followed closed behind for company. It was one of several she'd done of her photogenic daughter, and popular with the customers. Too bad she couldn't show the ones she'd done of the stranger a few nights ago. They were some of her best work. He'd taken most of the prints, but had missed a couple of the drawings she'd done in the back of her book. One was the picture she'd sketched that night. There was something about that drawing... Christy's stomach flipped every time she looked at it. He'd seemed so lonely out there on those rocks with the waves breaking below him and the sun setting on the horizon. She'd wanted to console him, hold him to her breast and tell him everything would be all right. That is until he'd opened his mouth and ruined the whole image.

"This nice picture. Your daughter?" the woman asked.

Christy nodded, her chest swelling with love. "She's four."

The elderly lady patted her arm. "Don't worry. She grow up fine."

Christy stiffened. "I'm sorry, I don't understand?" How could this stranger know anything of their situation?

The woman gazed at her and the knowledge in the wizened depths of her chocolate brown eyes was hard to deny. "Have faith, my child. All will be well one midnight clear."

With that cryptic comment, the woman turned and shuffled out of the store, nodding at the tall stranger who held the door. It was none other than Christy's merman.

***

Joel pushed open the glass door of *The Wandering Mind Studio* and frowned at the silver bells tinkling above his head. A stooped old lady gave him the once-over, then nodded and slipped past, leaving the scent of lavender and allspice in her wake. A group of Asians—four women and a man—followed close behind.

Joel took a couple of steps into the store before he saw the shadowy figure near the back wall. He was at a disadvantage coming in from the bright outdoor lighting to the cool dimness of the room and was unable to make out her features. It took a moment for his eyes to adjust and by then she was already on the move, putting space between them by stepping behind a waist-high glass counter running the length of the store.

"May I help you?" The husky tone of her voice prickled along his spine and made the hair on his arms—among other things—jump in response.

Annoyed, he ignored her and took the time to inspect the store's interior. And calm his body's betrayal.

The room was cluttered, filled with varying sizes of glass display cases. Some showcased pottery and native craftsmanship, while others exhibited porcelain dolls and west coast animals made from jade. The walls held framed prints, some in watercolor, others hand-drawn in pencil and crayon. Each an exquisite work of art. An all too familiar view of the breakwater had him swinging around in disbelief.

"You," he growled.

The woman stood with her arms crossed defensively, but the raised chin and flashing green eyes told him she'd already made the connection.

"What do you want?" she demanded. "How did you find me?"

"So you were telling the truth, you're not a reporter." He was tempted to smile at the inelegant snort his comment received. She really was a firecracker, this one.

"I believe I said that the other night. And speaking of stalking…" She raised her pencil-fine brow.

Two new customers entered, setting the bells tinkling again, and her demeanor turned warm and inviting. She glanced at him, hesitated, then strode around the counter to help the clients, her back ramrod straight.

Joel lingered, somewhat bemused. He couldn't remember the last time he'd been made to wait. More often than not, people were so ingratiating it maddened him. This was… refreshing.

Now that he could see her in the daylight she was quite pretty. Not beautiful. Her features were too narrow, her lips too wide. Yet something about her face was striking. Maybe it was those jade green eyes. They reminded him of the ocean in all its tumultuous glory. Or maybe it was the glorious crown of golden-red hair endowed with a life of its own, bouncing and shimmering halfway down her slim back. Her legs were long and athletic looking, encased in those narrow fitted track pants women seemed to favor these days. He'd always thought they looked ridiculous, until now.

He cleared his throat and turned away from the temptation of her curvy backside. Maybe he should just come back later when the owner returned. The last thing he needed to be doing right now was to get sidetracked by the prospect of the chase. Because that's all it was; once he won, his interest always disappeared.

"So, you never answered my question."

Her melodic voice floating from just over his shoulder startled him.

He swung around, surprised to see they were once again alone in the store. He hadn't even heard the blasted bells this time. She was shorter than he expected. Her spitfire personality had turned her into an Amazon in his mind.

"Where's your boss?" he asked, his tone somewhat abrupt but he couldn't help it, she threw him off-balance. "Aren't you rather young to be left running the store on your own?"

Her gaze lit with laughter. "Is that the best you've got?"

He looked at her, puzzled. "Best what?"

She tilted her head to the side as though trying to figure him out. "Forget it. Is there a message I can give my... boss for you?"

Joel had the insane urge to reach out and touch her to see if she was real. It was uncanny. She was the spitting image of his heroine. How could this have happened? He'd already written about Rebecca before meeting this woman on the beach the other night so that wasn't the reason. It made him supremely uncomfortable to look at her and feel like he knew what she was thinking—which of course he couldn't.

"Have we met before?" There had to be some explanation. Maybe she'd traveled to Scotland and he'd seen her there. Or maybe he'd lost his ever-lovin' mind. They say everyone has a doppelganger, but this... this was weird.

She laughed.

And no doubt thought him crazy.

"You mean other than our less than friendly meeting the other night? No, I don't think so."

Yeah, he didn't either.

He shook his head, suddenly eager to get home and do some editing. "Tell your boss her landlord was here."

He stepped out the door, but couldn't leave without gazing at her one more time. The shimmer in the glass when the door slid closed made her face waver, like an out of focus lens on a camera. A chill wormed its way down Joel's spine. He glanced at the cloudless blue of the December sky and tugged his jacket closed.

CHAPTER FIVE

Christy cursed the spark of mischief that more often than not landed her in trouble. Why hadn't she told him the truth? She watched as he bundled his coat and strode away, the sun picking out caramel highlights in his chocolate brown hair. Now that she'd seen him in the daylight, she realized he was even more attractive than before.

His accent for one—she waved her fingers in front of her face in a vain attempt to cool flushed cheeks—his Scottish brogue brushed against her skin in the most delicious way. It gave her shivers. And those eyes; a violet-blue that reminded her of sparkling twilight skies. His broad shoulders under the blue linen shirt and supple brown leather jacket accentuated a trim waist and legs in snug-fitting jeans and hiking boots.

Listen to her, waxing poetic when her whole life was about to go down the toilet. The moment he found out who she really was they may as well start packing their bags. He'd never believe her reasons for the late rent payments now.

What was she going to do?

She locked the front entrance, posted the back in an hour sign, then strode to the door leading to a short hall opening into the living quarters at the rear of the old house. The building was a two-story, turreted, Victorian heritage home crafted in the late eighteen hundreds. She'd fallen in love with the snowy white gingerbread trim and hardwood flooring. It reminded her of a dollhouse she'd played with as a child. If only they could stay.

Jill was laying on her tummy coloring. She glanced up at the sound of the door and a smile broke the look of extreme concentration on her pixie face.

"Mommy," she sang, lifting Christy's heart. "Look, I'm an artist too." She held up a picture of two killer whales jumping high above the dancing waves of the Pacific Ocean. The color and composition of the drawing were remarkable; but then Christy was prejudiced.

"That's lovely, honey," she said, and drew her daughter into a strawberry-scented hug. "Don't forget to sign your name at the bottom. You can't get famous otherwise."

Jill giggled and tipped her head back, her long, curly hair sweeping Christy's hands wrapped around her waist. "What's famous mean, Mommy?"

Christy brushed a kiss across her freckled nose. "Well, it's when everyone knows your name and wants to meet you."

Jill digested the explanation for a moment, then a mischievous light entered her eyes. "Is that when I'll get to go to Katy's for a sleepover?"

A lump the size of a baseball lodged in Christy's throat. She'd known Jill was disappointed when her friend had a birthday sleepover and she couldn't stay, but obviously it bothered her more than she'd let on. Her beautiful, brave little girl.

She cleared her throat and gave her daughter a playful pat on the backside. "I guess we'll find out when you're a celebrity. Until then, it's time to wash your hands and do a reading before lunch. Did you decide what you'd like to eat?"

Jill rubbed her bum, ever the drama queen, and looked at her crayon-covered fingers. "Grilled cheese. Aunty Claire is already making it. They're clean, see?"

"Jill Marie Taylor, go and wash. I want to hear the birthday song, missy." Christy shook her head as Jill headed for the bathroom, her steps dragging like she was going to the gallows. What was it with kids and water?

She crouched and picked up the loose crayons, fitting them back in their box, then set everything on the stool in front of the green and gold plaid armchair. Circling the matching sofa she headed to the kitchen. The brocade wallpaper and dark wood flooring creaked and groaned beneath her feet and made Christy dream of empire waist dresses with crinolines and fancy hats. Gentlemen callers with bouquets of flowers stopping by to leave their card in the hope the pretty maiden of the house will grant them favors. Not that she wanted any callers, whether they be gentlemen, or gruff, sexy Heathcliff types who just happened to be her landlord.

Claire turned, a spatula in her hand, at the sound of her entrance. "Goodness, is it that time already? I've almost got lunch ready. Sit down and relax." She expertly flipped a sandwich in the pan and set the other out for cutting. "How was your morning?"

Christy opened the refrigerator and emerged with a quart of milk. She poured enough for each of them, careful to measure Jill's just to the line marked on the glass. "Busy. With Christmas on the way, we're getting more tourists coming through."

Claire brought the plates of food to the table and took a seat, smiling wryly at the milk. "You're bound and determined to make me healthy, aren't you?" Before Christy could tell her yet again why milk was an important part of a daily diet, she took a big drink, grimacing only a little. "That's great news, child.

See? I told you to have some faith and everything would work out in the end. God hears your prayers."

Yeah? If that were true why did he bestow a horrible, life-threatening disease on her little girl? And leave her all alone to deal with it? Where was Claire's God when Christy cried every time she had to poke her daughter's tiny fingers, or when her blood sugars suddenly dropped and she almost passed out in the middle of the night? Where was He when the pediatrician warned her Jill would be susceptible to infection, and regular checkups were needed because her other organs could be affected? That there was no cure, and a high mortality rate without close twenty-four-seven supervision? It seemed more likely God only heard what he wanted to hear, and helped those he wanted to help. She wasn't part of that club.

Not wishing to get into a philosophical conversation guaranteed to cause dissention, Christy murmured a non-committal remark and called for Jill. "Okay, punkin, lunch is served."

Jill came skipping into the kitchen, all sunshine and rainbows, her disgruntled demeanor a thing of the past. "Yay, thanks, Aunty. I love grilled cheese sandwiches."

Claire and Christy shared an amused look. "That and cheese pizzas," Christy agreed, though pizza was a rare treat since Jill developed T1D. "Let's do your reading and key in the carbs so you can bolus, then you can eat."

Well used to the routine after almost two years, Jill held out her hand and waited, still humming the birthday song. Her breath hitched for a millisecond at the prick to her finger, but then it was over… for her at least.

Claire patted Christy's back and helped Jill into her chair. The two chatted about Christmas presents and decorating the tree while Christy set the monitor to deliver insulin to the pod on Jill's arm. Somehow, she had to find the money to get Jill the puppy she'd been asking for since forever. She hadn't read the lease yet, but doubtless that was another issue the landlord was going to hold against her. If it wasn't for the almost impossible odds of finding another place that fit their needs quite so perfectly, Christy would consider moving. But they had settled here now. It was home. And she planned on doing whatever it took to stay.

CHAPTER SIX

Joel was grateful for one thing at least; his meeting with the young woman at the art shop had struck his muse. By the time he arrived back home, his fingers were literally itching to tap dance with the computer's keyboard.

Three days and some thirty thousand words later, he came up for air. He leaned back and stretched, grimacing at the kinks in his shoulders and neck. The intense satisfaction with the way the story had headed was only slightly diminished by the growl of his gut and the bristle of his new beard. Time to get cleaned up and find something to eat.

An hour later he'd showered and shaved, checked the fridge, though he knew it was empty, and called his grandmother to go for lunch.

"So, you are alive. I was beginning to wonder." Her tart voice coming down the line made him feel like a child again.

He chuckled. "Sorry, Grannie, I was on a roll. Had to strike while the iron was hot, don't ya know."

She sighed. "You sound just like your da. I guess since you're buying me lunch, I can forgive you. Where do you want to meet?"

"I can pick you up. I wanted to stop in and see my tenant anyway." He picked his keys out of the bowl by the door.

"No," she said, her tone a bit breathless. "I have a wee one I'm taking care of. You probably don't want her feet all over that fancy new car of yours. How about Floyd's? You loved that place as a youngster."

What was she doing with a child? He hoped someone wasn't taking advantage of her generous spirit and making her into a glorified nanny or something. She should be enjoying her retirement years, not raising another family's kids.

"I'll see you there. Drive safe," he warned, well aware of her propensity to speed.

She laughed. "Bye, son. See you in a few minutes."

She laughed, but he was serious. He was surprised she still had her license... or did she?

He was about to step out the door when the bell rang. *It better not be a salesman...* It wasn't. The woman who had haunted his dreams—or at least her spitting image—stood on his doorstep, a determined smile planted on those kissable lips.

***

Christy hid a gasp and kept the smile pinned even though her cheeks hurt. It should be illegal to look that good. He didn't even have to work for it, dammit.

His hair was ruffled as though he'd forgotten to comb it this morning and decided to just run his fingers through it instead. He wore a dress shirt tucked into dark trousers with the sleeves rolled halfway up muscular forearms. The contrast between his deeply tanned skin with its light dusting of gold-tipped hairs and the stark whiteness of the material made her pulse flutter.

The man was lethal.

Her hands wcre sweaty, her heart was a runaway train, and every careful thought she'd planned to say had fled from her brain.

"What are you doing here?" He blocked the doorway with his big body, suspicion turning his eyes a stormy blue-gray.

The guy had serious stalker issues. There was therapy for that. The random thought eased her own tension and her smile turned genuine. "I followed you home the other day. I've been camped out by that tree hoping to see you," she waved a hand toward a tall Arbutus, "but now I just need the bathroom. Do you mind?"

She pushed her way under the arm raised against the doorframe, and tried not to notice how very male he smelled.

"Hey." He turned and filled the foyer with his presence. "You can't just go barging in wherever you want. I should call the cops."

She hesitated, then shrugged. In for a penny, in for a pound, her mom always used to say. "Go ahead. While you're at it, which way to the washroom?" She really did need to go, a combination of nerves and too much coffee this morning.

He growled something vulgar and pointed down the hall.

Christy nodded and hurried to close the bathroom door on his scowling face. She needed to regroup, and fast. What was she thinking, coming here and bearding the lion in his den? The plan when she'd left home had seemed so simple. Drive over, butter him up a bit, *then* casually drop into the conversation she was his missing tenant. She opened her purse and counted out the crisp hundred dollar bills for about the tenth time since the sale of one of her larger watercolors. The money would have come in handy to catch up overdo bills and maybe give her poor car an oil change, but it would have to wait. No home, no business. At least now they'd have a roof over their heads until after Christmas. She'd worry about the rest later.

Gathering her courage in both hands, Christy reapplied the mulberry lipstick she'd chosen for the occasion, tucked a few stray hairs, and yanked the door open fully expecting a face-to-face with her nemesis.

The hall was empty.

She knew she should wait there, but curiosity pushed her forward, and she ventured into the lion's domain.

The house was neater than she expected. Maybe he had a wife or girlfriend who cleaned for him, and why that thought caused a pang in her breast she wasn't going to contemplate. She barely knew the man. Just because he appealed to her on a visceral level meant nothing at all. Besides, his acerbic attitude was enough to drive any woman crazy. She should offer his wife an award for putting up with him.

She moved a little slower, half expecting some fishwife to pop up and chew her out for having the nerve to chase her man. Not that she was. Chasing, that is. The only plan on her mind was to pay said man, offer another apology for the unintentional subterfuge, and hopefully put all of this behind them.

Oh yeah, and ask about a puppy for Jill.

Easy, peasey.

A tension headache narrowed both her gaze and her temperament. Where the heck did he go? She was about to call his name when she heard a noise on the second floor.

Did he want her to meet him upstairs? She'd caught a glimpse of the large glassed-in solarium when she'd parked, but surely he could have waited to escort her through the house?

Nerves tightening, Christy started the climb. She hoped he wasn't some kind of pervert waiting to tug her into his bedroom and have his way with her. The image of that dark head lowering to her breast caused her stomach muscles, and lower, to clench. Her lips firmed. She was a modern day, independent woman. Where were these notions of getting swept off her feet by some sort of scoundrel coming from? Too many romance novels. That was her excuse, and she was sticking with it.

The house had to be as old as the one she was renting, but where hers was frills and lace, this was more like dark suits and stuffed shirts. The staircase was narrow and followed a slight curve that left the upper regions hidden from view. The higher she climbed, the more nervous she became. This was a bad idea, very bad.

"Hello?" she said, and frowned at her quivery voice. "Hello, is anyone up here?" She hesitated on the top tread, not sure whether to keep going, or turn tail and run.

A dark head appeared not two feet away, from a doorway she'd missed in the shadows. Christy screeched and jumped back, except she'd forgotten about the stairs. Her arms flailed in a helpless attempt to save herself.

Just as she overbalanced and started to fall, a rough masculine hand reached out and pulled her to safety.

CHAPTER SEVEN

Joel's arms were filled with warm, willing woman and he couldn't catch a breath. His heart hadn't caught up to the fact she was safe, and was threatening to jump right out of his chest. That was too close to a disaster.

"Are you nuts?" he growled, pumped with adrenaline.

She stiffened and broke free with an indignant huff. "Of course not. Is it my fault you had to scare the heck out of me?"

He wasn't sure which he regretted more; his outburst or his empty arms. "I yelled and told you where I was." He watched her still pale face turn and take in their surroundings in dawning wonder. He knew the feeling. The solarium was his favorite room in the house—his escape.

"Ever hear of lights?" she said absently, wandering over to the glass. "It's that little switch on the wall."

"You're a barrel of laughs." He admired the effect of the sun on her strawberry blond hair, and the outline of her slim figure and generous breasts under a flowery white dress. "You want to tell me again why you're here, in my house."

She peeked at him over her shoulder, then turned back to the window. "I came to tell you the truth," she murmured.

Okaay.

She had his attention. He glanced at his watch, aware that he needed to get going before Grannie thought she'd been stood up. "How about we start with your name? I don't think I heard it the other day."

She swung around and crossed her arms over a suitcase-sized handbag draped cross-body over her chest. He absolutely wasn't noticing how the strap tightened the material hugging her breasts. Nope, not him.

"It's Christy," she blurted, chin in the air. "Christy Taylor."

It took a moment for the words to compute. *Well, shit.*

Of all the women he could be attracted to, why did it have to be his troublesome tenant?

He shook his head. He should have known. Fate liked playing these kinds of games with him. "Did you come to explain why you're almost two months late with rent? Or maybe you planned on hurting yourself in my home so that I wouldn't chance kicking you out of your house." He slammed the door, sealing them into the room. "C'mon then, which is it?"

Her eyes flashed green fire and a becoming flush of pink traveled from the two undone buttons on the top of her dress, up her neck, and turned her cheeks rosy. Too bad it was caused by anger instead of desire.

"You," she sputtered. "You really are an arrogant son-of-a-gun aren't you?" She tugged the bag over her head, dug around inside and came up with a wad of cash clenched in her hand. Resentment in every line of her body, she stomped over and shoved the bills at his chest.

"Here, take your damn blood money. And don't worry, my daughter and I will find somewhere else to live before next month."

Joel stood there, slightly stunned. She had quite the temper. He was too slow to react and before he could lift his hand to take the money, she let go. The bills drifted to the floor like confetti, but his attention was on the woman, not the cash. She'd already returned to her purse, bending over to grab it off the floor, and affording him a glimpse of toned thighs. Head high, she stamped toward the door in ridiculously high red heels, obviously planning to leave on that dramatic note.

Joel couldn't help it. He clapped.

"You sure you're not an actress?"

That stopped her in her tracks.

She swung around and eyed him like he was something she'd stepped in at the dog park.

"What is your problem?" she asked.

He wasn't sure how to answer that. Other than the fact she threw him off-balance, and he had the strongest urge to toss her over his shoulder and take her to bed… there were no problems.

"I don't know what you mean."

She came back to poke a finger at his chest. "Ever since we met, you've been giving me the gears."

Poke.

"I'm sorry I drew your sacred body."

Poke.

"And I'm sorry I was late with the rent, but you could at least have the decency to let me explain."

Poke, poke.

"Ouch." He scowled and grabbed hold of her hand. "Quit that."

Joel gazed into the mysterious green pools of her eyes and did the only thing he could.

He kissed her.

***

Christy's mouth was open, about to shoot streams of vitriol at the man who had turned into her enemy, when his head descended. Warm, faintly minty breath combined with firm lips and turned her world inside out. She went from mad to feverish in an instant. He was like nothing she'd ever tasted before. Every thought drained away. His kiss became the center of the universe.

Brawny hands cupped the sides of her face, angling her head to receive his attention. Heat poured from his body, so near she could feel his chest brushing hers, sensitizing her nipples to the point of near pain. She pressed closer, desperate to ease the ache, and reveled in the groan that escaped his lips. She ran trembling fingers across broad shoulders and an even wider chest. His well-defined pectoral muscles under the soft material of his shirt made her feel cocooned, safe in the harbor of his arms. Dangerous dreams of them as a couple danced through her mind, even as she realized the folly of such thoughts. This was a stolen moment. One she could enjoy, then tuck away, to be revisited on those lonely nights of her future.

"You taste like satin and sin," he whispered. His lips left hers to travel the length of her jaw. His teeth nipped lightly at her ear, and when she gasped, he kissed it better.

She shivered; filled with a hunger she hadn't felt in a long, long while. He tempted her. More than was wise.

"We'd better stop," she sighed. *Before I can't.*

He nuzzled the side of her neck, not playing fair, then slowly stepped back, his gaze heated as it searched her face.

"You sure?"

Hell, no.

There was nothing she'd like better than an irresponsible afternoon spent with this man, but… her life didn't have room for more problems.

And Joel Carpenter was one big complication.

CHAPTER EIGHT

Joel ended up almost three quarters of an hour late to his lunch with Grannie. He'd needed time to get his shit together after Christy stormed through the front door and proceeded to turn his life upside down. She confused him. He didn't know what to do with her. The safe choice would be to help her find another place to rent, get her settled, and close the door on their non-relationship. And if it were only a simple sexual attraction between them, maybe that's what he would have done, but something held him back.

From their first meeting, when he'd taken her for a sensation-seeking journalist, he'd been drawn to her flashing eyes and sarcastic tongue that lured even as it aggravated him. She had spunk. Joel wanted to know what made her tick.

Grannie was at the back of the restaurant, sitting in a booth with James Dean smiling down on her. She glanced pointedly at the clock, then back to him, and he knew he wasn't going to get off easy.

"Sorry, Gran, unexpected company, I'm afraid." He leaned down and kissed a leathery cheek. "My apologies."

He started to slide into the seat across from her and almost collided with a little girl staring at him with big green eyes and a serious face. He hovered, unsure, then sat on the edge of the bench, leaving plenty of room between them. Kids made him uncomfortable, not that he'd been around many. They were too... small. He always felt like a bull in a china shop around them.

"Have you been waiting long?" he asked Grannie, aware of the child watching his every move. He forced himself not to fidget.

"Hmm, a while, yes. We've already had lunch. Jill here," Gran smiled at the girl, "is on a strict schedule so we couldn't delay for long, but you go ahead. We were just thinking of sharing some ice cream, weren't we, Jill?"

The child's gaze shifted and Joel sighed under his breath. Now he knew how those bugs felt under the microscope.

"Thanks, Aunty Claire." Her voice slid under his skin, soft and way too polite for a young child. "Can you pass my kit?"

He watched curiously as Grannie passed a black travel bag over the table. Instead of the expected doll collection, or coloring paraphernalia, the girl pulled a little black canvas bag out and withdrew some kind of device. A stab of sympathy pierced his heart when he realized she held a blood glucose monitor. She was diabetic.

She used the tester to poke her middle finger. Joel flinched. The hair on his arms stood on end and all but tried to run from the restaurant. He hated needles. How she did that so matter-of-factly… his respect soared.

"Do you need help, honey?" Grannie squinted across the table while searching her multi-compartment purse for her glasses.

Jill shook her head and sent her pigtails flying. "I got it. Mommy taught me how." She carefully touched the test strip in the machine to the drop of bright red blood welling up on the end of her finger. They all focused on the monitor's display and waited for the beep to tell her reading.

"How much should I do for the ice cream?" she asked Grannie.

"Just a minute, I'm looking it up," Grannie answered, her glasses now perched on the end of her nose as she thumbed through information on her phone.

Joel sat back and watched the two of them—one so young, the other aging—and his throat tightened. He'd always taken his own health for granted, never worried about other's issues as long as they didn't affect him. He donated to a few charities to ease his conscience and that was enough.

Until now.

Something about the little girl's bravery ripped a hole in his heart that wouldn't be easy to close.

"Want some?" she asked, sliding her half-full bowl towards him with an uncertain smile that showed a couple of crooked teeth.

He looked at her, legs swinging gently back and forth under the table. She had the faintest sprinkle of freckles across the bridge of her nose and reminded him of those ceramic dolls Grannie used to collect when he was a child. A pang tightened his chest.

"Where are your parents?" he asked, shaking his head at the ice cream.

She gazed at him like he'd kicked her dog or something. Oh shit, were they…?

"Her father lives in Alberta," Grannie said, shooting him an I-taught-you-better-than-that glare. "And her mom…"

"Is right here," came a harried voice from behind them. "Sorry I'm late, I had to… You," Christy said as she came even with the table. "What are *you* doing here?"

She was no more surprised than he was. What were the chances…? Never mind. The way his luck ran, he should have known.

"Hello again," he murmured, standing to let her slide in beside her daughter. He should have realized who her mother was. Now, with their strawberry blond heads close as Christy gave her little girl a hug and a kiss, it became obvious.

Envy flared. He ached to be part of a unit like theirs. He'd never had the familial care of a loving family. His parents had been too busy with their own lives—one a doctor, the other a professor—to bother with a troublesome young boy. Without his grandparents' guidance, he hated to think what he might have become.

Joel turned to Grannie and met her quizzical gaze.

"You two know each other?" she asked.

He glanced at Christy and got the warning look. Jill's curious gaze was turning nervous, as though she had picked up on the developing tension.

He gave her a reassuring wink, and turned back to Grannie. "Not really, no. We just met today when she delivered her rent." An almost truth. They *had* officially met today—mouth to mouth.

Time to go, before he landed himself into trouble.

"It was nice meeting you, Jill," he bowed slightly, and smiled at her giggle. The smile flat-lined when he met Christy's wounded gaze. "I hope you'll reconsider your decision. You're welcome to stay in the house until you find something better."

"Are we moving?" Jill whined. "I don't wanna. I like it here, Mommy."

She shot him a *you're-a-dickhead* glare, which he kind of was, and turned to assure her daughter they would be fine.

He looked to Grannie for support, and was hurt by the sad reproach shining from her faded blue eyes.

Stomach churning with self-disgust, Joel turned and headed out the door.

CHAPTER NINE

Christy stared at the woman who had become like a mother to her and fought to harness the sense of betrayal twisting her stomach into knots. "Why didn't you tell me he was your grandson?"

Claire turned away from her contemplation of Joel's departing back, her cloudy gaze contrite behind bifocal lenses.

"At first I didn't realize you two had met, and then after I saw one of your drawings and found out he was your beach encounter…." She shrugged and fiddled with the spoon on the side of her teacup. "I didn't think you would want me to keep taking care of your girl and I would have hated that. She makes me feel young again." She smiled sadly at Jill enjoying her dish of ice cream.

The anger drained, leaving behind an uncomfortable silence. Christy hated to think Claire would consider her so shallow. It was true she was hurt by her friend's subterfuge, but never dreamed of cutting the other woman out of their lives. Jill loved her like a grandmother. She was an important part of their family. It was just too bad she had to be related to… him.

She stretched across and caught Claire's age-spotted hand in hers. "I'm sorry."

She squeezed for a moment and let go, glancing down to see how much Big Ears was taking in. Thankfully she was too busy enjoying the rare treat to bother with the adults.

"It just caught me off-guard when I saw you two together. I don't exactly have a good relationship with your grandson, as you know." She hoped the pink staining her cheeks would be taken for the warm restaurant. "Anyway, we'll be moving soon, so it's a moot point. I hope you know you'll always be welcome, wherever we are."

"I'll talk to Joel. He's a good boy, I'm sure he didn't mean what he said." Claire began to dig through the many zippered compartments of her handbag until she came up with her cell phone.

"No, don't," Christy implored.

Her hands turned sweaty just thinking of Joel's reaction. The noise of happy diners, and that of a boy only a couple of years older than Jill slamming the saloon doors leading to the restrooms so hard they almost hit the wall, grated on her stretched nerves. Joel would think she'd coerced Claire into making the call, and besides, she wasn't sure she'd stay even if they reached a compromise. It would be too embarrassing. She couldn't believe he'd accused her of trying to stage an accident in his home. And then she'd actually let him kiss her. Was she nuts?

It was his fault. Hypnotism was the only explanation. She couldn't be attracted to him. He was everything she abhorred in a man.

Arrogant.

Annoying.

Overbearing.

But, she had to admit he was also kind and loving to his grandmother. Handsome enough to make her pulse jump. And yet, somehow… isolated. It was the last that got to her the most. Christy knew all about loneliness. Her life, even before the divorce, had been lonely. Kevin often spent long hours at work and when he finally did come home it was to disappear into his office until bedtime. Sex was the only common ground they'd shared those last few years. When they lost that too, there was no more reason to stay.

She'd sworn never to go down the physical attraction road again. Her life was complicated enough without riding that roller coaster. Some distance between herself and Mr. Personality was for the best. She just needed to convince her hormones that she was right.

"Mommy, where did the nice man go?" Jill's warble interrupted her musings.

Christy looked at the nearly empty bowl of ice cream instead of her daughter. "Did you bolus for your dessert?"

Jill had a hard time accepting her father didn't live with them any more. He may not have been the best husband, but worse than that was his aloofness with his daughter. She'd tried so hard to gain her daddy's approval—it broke Christy's heart. Men weren't worth the stress.

Jill's cheeks reddened. She knew desserts were for special days, darn it.

"Uh, huh. Aunty Claire and Joel were sharing with me." *So don't be mad*, her expression seemed to say.

"That's Mr. Carpenter to you, young lady. And we'll talk about your food choices when we get home." She hated playing the hard-ass with her daughter, but when it came to her health there was no choice.

Jill heaved a put-upon sigh and pushed the bowl away before going back to coloring the fireman on the children's menu.

Christy bit down on tears and gave her a quick peck on the cheek. For the most part Jill handled the changes better than she did. And thank God for that.

"Joel is fine. He'd look for his father if you called him anything else," Claire said. She nodded toward the ice cream treat. "That was my fault. I thought if we shared…"

"It's fine," Christy murmured. "She just has to learn what to watch out for. We won't always be around." She smiled her thanks to a young girl in hipster jeans and tie-dyed top who poured her coffee, then spun away to help a group of teenaged boys laughing and shoving each other as they filed into another booth. Had she ever been that young and carefree? Not that she could remember. Her family had emphasized the importance of good grades, so while her friends were out hanging around together, she'd been hard at work on calculus and biology.

She shook off the past and refocused on the woman across the table. Claire looked exhausted. There were dark shadows under her eyes, and her already small frame seemed more diminutive somehow. Maybe taking care of Jill was too much for her friend. And if so, what was she going to do? There weren't many caregivers qualified or whom she'd trust to watch her daughter. As soon as the thought crossed her mind, Christy cursed her selfishness.

"Are you feeling okay? You look like a stiff breeze would blow you over."

Claire startled, then gave a forced laugh. She picked up an indigo crayon and started to color in the sky on Jill's paper. "Course I'm okay. Nothing keeps us Michaels down for long." She glanced at Christy, then went back to shading the sky. "It's flu season and I didn't want to chance getting sick and passing it on," she nodded to Jill's bent head. "So I got the shot a couple days ago. They warn everyone you might have a few symptoms of the flu afterward, but it shouldn't be serious. Guess I'm testing their theory."

Christy clicked her tongue in dismay. "Why didn't you say something? You should be home in bed." She started to gather up their belongings, anxious to get Claire home to rest.

Claire reached across and stopped her movement. "Relax. Another ten minutes won't make a difference one way or another. Besides," she said, her eyes taking on a mischievous glow, "I want to know what happened between you and my grandson this afternoon."

Looking into the other woman's knowing gaze, Christy squirmed. How was she going to explain the unexplainable?

CHAPTER TEN

Christy concentrated on the broad strokes of her pencil as she labored to get the shading just right. She'd been working on this piece for almost a week and it was close to completion. Seeing the finished product for the first time was her second favorite part of being an artist, but it didn't compare to the rush of that first slash of color on paper. The excitement of the unknown was addictive. She couldn't imagine her life without art, though Kevin had done his level best to weed it out of her.

"It's not dignified. What will the others say?"

He spent more time worrying about the *others* than his family. It was all about appearance with him, and Jill's "defect," as he called it, was simply unacceptable.

So they left.

She stared at the sheets of rain she'd created tumbling off the roof of the old Victorian mansion, and felt a shiver of foreboding. Silly, of course. It was only a drawing. But that didn't stop her from closing the sketchpad and setting everything away.

She wandered over to check on Jill napping on a settee in the guest lounge of the store. Claire still wasn't feeling herself, and neither of them wanted to chance Jill getting sick, so Christy was keeping her in the store as a shop assistant for the time being.

The silver bells above the door chimed and she turned to see Joel entering, his head and shoulders damp from the west coast rain.

Her heart kicking into overdrive, she bent to tuck the covers around Jill and count back from ten before facing him.

She should have counted from fifty.

The angles of his face stood in stark relief against the dark canvas of seal wet hair he carelessly brushed back, the ends dampening his collar. The chill outside gave his cheeks a ruddy flush that highlighted the violet hues in his blue eyes. Dazzling eyes. Fine-looking man.

Until those gorgeous lips spoke.

"What did you do to my grandmother?"

Christy shook her head, sure she must have misheard. "What are you talking about?"

He let the door close, muffling the sound of the rain hitting the puddles forming on the pavement.

"I just came from her house, she looks like shit." He glanced at Jill, hesitated, and lowered his voice. "She said something about flu shots and the kid there, and no, she wasn't going to the doctors, even though I threatened her." His worry was as obvious as his frustration.

Christy softened. She couldn't fault the man for caring, even if he could use some lessons in showing it.

"I'm sorry Claire is sick. I don't like it any more than you do, I tried to get her to go in, but she's stubborn." She poured a cup of coffee and raised an enquiring eyebrow. He gave a short nod and stepped closer, too close for her peace of mind. "Wonder where she gets that from?"

Their fingers touched when she passed over his cup and Christy's pulse bounced around in her veins like a pinball game. She let go so fast the liquid sloshed, coming dangerously near to breaching the rim of the cup.

Awkward this close to him, she turned away on the pretext of adding some sugar to her own cup, though she certainly didn't need any more stimulants. The air was filled with the intoxicating scent of rain and the damp leather from his jacket. Christy had the insane urge to bury her nose in the open v of his dress shirt. To lick the moisture that clung to his skin, to taste again the dark desire of his lips.

"Are you okay?"

His voice coming from right behind her made Christy jump. Her gaze rebounded off his before she stepped away, eager to put some space between them.

"Of course, I'm okay. Why would you ask that?" Did he know she had a crush on him? Oh, God, how embarrassing.

"You look kind of flushed." He followed her and before she could stop him, cupped a hand to her cheek. "You're burning up."

Her eyelids slid closed for a second, the better to take in the calloused warmth of his touch. When they opened it was to see his gaze fixed on her mouth and she realized she'd been sucking on her bottom lip. She let go with a soft pop and his gaze darkened to cobalt.

"It's not because of the flu," she whispered.

Joel smiled, acknowledging her words. He set his cup on the counter, then took hers with slow deliberation and set it down too, meeting her bemused gaze. "Before one of us gets burned."

As his mouth lowered, Christy had a feeling it was too late for that.

***

Joel stared at the plush fullness of Christy's lips and wondered if he was the one catching the flu. Hot and cold shivers chased each other over his chest and arms and his knees would have caved in if they weren't locked together, somehow holding him upright and swaying toward his objective; tasting the honeyed sweetness of her mouth. Ever since they'd kissed last week he couldn't eat, could barely sleep. She was on his mind so constantly he'd begun to think he'd dreamed the whole encounter.

But no, she was real, and right here where he could fill up on her sumptuous body until the cravings were over and he could go back to his solitary life in peace. With her shimmering green eyes and whiskey-colored hair she reminded him of the mythical sirens he'd read about as a child, luring men to a watery grave.

She fascinated him, this woman who refused to bow to adversity. Grannie had informed him of her story after giving him what-for over the rent issue. If Christy would have just explained when she came to his house… instead she'd climbed onto her high-horse and hadn't even given him a chance.

Her eyelids fluttered and her mouth parted on a soft sigh that feathered across his lips and caused an internal combustion. He knew they should talk out their differences, but at the moment he could barely hang onto his name, much less anything else.

He slid his thumb across her lower lip with just enough pressure to make it plump, and groaned when her tongue slipped out and caressed his skin. He just needed one little…

Their mouths were a millimeter apart when a young voice chirped, "What's wrong, Mommy? Is there somethin' in your eye?"

Joel closed his eyes and swallowed his disappointment before looking down at the child tugging on his pant leg.

"Are you helping Mommy, Joel?"

I'd like to.

He grimaced, at a loss for words. Christy's eyes had opened in stunned surprise. She looked at him with dawning horror, then down at her daughter with her hand gripping the material of his trousers. The absurdity of the situation must have struck her because her lips quirked with a humor she invited him to share. And he might have, if she hadn't dropped in a crouch too near his aching dick for comfort.

"Yes, honey, Joel was… helping mommy. How about we let him drink his coffee in peace and go find you a snack?"

Joel watched the two of them traipse off to the rear of the house and wondered how he could have fallen so far, so fast.

CHAPTER ELEVEN

Christy bundled Jill up in her winter rain jacket and gathered the bag filled with snacks, juice, testing strips, insulin, and the hundred and one other things that came with getting ready to be away from home for a few hours with a young child. Sometimes she missed the freedom of her younger years before having children, but she would never regret giving birth to her girl. Jill was her world.

Today they were off to watch the Truck Parade, followed by the Lighted Ship Parade right after. She wanted to get there early to find the best spot for Jill to see the floats. Claire was meeting someone downtown for lunch and planned to meet them at the inner harbor so Christy didn't have to go out of her way to pick her up.

Jill had been bouncing off the walls all day. "Is it time yet?"

"No, honey. Not for a while," Christy said, busy washing the morning's dishes.

A couple hours later Jill came skipping into the store, delighting a couple of seniors shopping for gifts. "Is it time yet?"

"Not yet. I'll tell you when." Christy smiled at her daughter and ruffled her hair.

They were late sitting down to lunch.

"Is it time yet?" Jill asked, her mouth full of her favorite grilled cheese sandwich.

"Jill!" Christy warned, pointing to her mouth. "No talking with your mouth full." And then, before she could ask again, "And yes, it's time. As soon as you finish your lunch."

Her excitement contagious, Christy's own steps had a spring to them as they left the car parked near one of the tall-masted ships anchored in the harbor getting ready for the evening's events. There was plenty of laughter and singing on deck and she smiled in response. The air was brisk with a hint of moisture overlaid with the aroma of kelp and brine. She inhaled deeply, appreciating the scent. There was something about the ocean that fed her soul.

"Look, Mommy, there's Claire." Jill pointed and tried to slip the grip Christy had on her fingers. Christy made sure the coast was clear between them before letting her go. Jill didn't always pay attention when her mind was on something and tended to overlook anyone in her way. She'd almost been mowed down more than once in big crowds so now Christy erred on the side of caution.

Claire waved and bent over, opening her arms to catch Jill to her bosom. The two had grown so close, it caused a pang in her heart to think of having to move away from here. She'd searched online and left her number with numerous realtors, but the market was tight and there was very little to find in an affordable rental.

Oh well, time enough to worry about that later, today was about having fun with her daughter. She smiled and picked up her pace, only to come to a staggering halt when a tall man stepped out from the shadow of the tourist shops lining the waterfront.

Joel.

What was he doing here?

Dismay warred with exhilaration, the resulting discord compounded by the cacophony of noise caused by the seagulls squawking overhead.

The shock of seeing him again so soon after their disastrous non-kiss left her discombobulated. He'd been gone when they returned from getting Jill a snack the other day, so this was the first she'd seen him since. At the time she'd been relieved he'd left— or at least that's what she told herself. Truth was, she wished they'd had five more minutes to test the waters, so to speak.

He made her feel… things. Emotions she hadn't felt in a very long time. Dangerous desires she didn't know what to do with. And what about him? He wanted her, that much was obvious. But Christy wasn't interested in a quick hook-up, her life was messed up enough without adding to the mix. Even if he were interested in a relationship—which he'd made no suggestion of—how could she when she didn't even know where they would be living next month?

No, it was better to back away now, before either of them got hurt. She rubbed at the ache in her breast.

***

Joel saw Christy's hesitation and cursed the fact he was the cause of her distress. He'd told Grannie he shouldn't come, but she had insisted.

"Joel Francis Carpenter, how often do I ask you to do something?" She'd stared at him with reproof shining from her watery eyes. "I don't get to see you near enough as is, what with you off writing the novel of the century and all." She smiled and hugged his arm. "C'mon, honey, it'll do you good."

What could he say to that?

So here he was, and there she was, and Grannie would have some 'splainin' to do when they got home.

Christy looked gorgeous. The late afternoon light hitting her hair turned it to a fiery nimbus around her head. She wore one of the flowing gypsy skirts she seemed to prefer, rain boots on her feet. Her jacket was a tight-fitting chocolate brown suede with a band of fringes that showed off her generous cleavage. Give her a tambourine and a pair of gold hoop earrings and she'd fit right into a Romanian countryside.

He glanced down at his Salvatore Ferragamo Oxfords and his freshly pressed suit pants. She was sunshine and apple pies and he was cloudy nights and stormy seas. The two didn't mix. He should make an excuse and leave, let them enjoy the parade without him. But then he glanced down at the kid in Grannie's arms and he couldn't say the words. Her enthusiasm in the upcoming event shone from her pixie face. Her thin body fairly vibrated with excitement and Joel craved to be a part of it. After years of solitude this little girl—he looked up as Christy joined them—and her mother had broken the seal he'd wrapped around his heart.

He felt invigorated. Energized. Powerless to fight the feelings these two engendered.

He didn't even want to try.

Now he just had to convince her to give him a chance.

CHAPTER TWELVE

Christy gazed in awe at the splendor of the two-story blue and white decorated Christmas tree in the lobby of the elegant hotel. Piped holiday music added to the festive feel as families made a tour of the marble foyer and grand staircase to the second floor where more trees stood on display.

She smiled and waved when Jill peeked through the railings above, her eyes shining with laughter. She'd attached herself to Joel from the moment they'd arrived. Christy met Joel's lopsided grin and her heart fluttered. Kevin was missing out on knowing his sweet, beautiful little girl.

"That's my favorite song," Claire said, swaying back and forth to the tune of Silver Bells. The multitude of balls and lights on the tree twinkled and glowed, turning the whole scene into a magical wonderland.

A well-groomed couple stood nearby waiting their turn to register for a suite. The woman wore diamonds and furs as though they were jeans and beads, while the gentleman was decked out in a three-piece suit that probably cost more than Christy's car.

It wasn't that she missed the wealth that came with being Kevin's wife, so much as she did miss having a companion, someone to talk to late at night. Someone to hold her in his arms.

The counter became free and the man led his wife over to sign in. It wasn't until they turned to follow the porter that Christy noticed the swell of the woman's tummy. They would be parents soon; what a lovely Christmas gift that would be.

"He looks happy," Claire murmured, her tone laced with satisfaction.

Christy turned from her contemplation of the couple and watched Jill traipse down the stairs, Joel following close behind. The couple had neared the staircase themselves now, and she held her breath, praying Jill watched where she was going. Of course she didn't, too busy gawking at all the sights and sounds to notice the pregnant woman in her path.

Christy started forward, knowing there was little chance of stopping the impending catastrophe, but determined to try anyway. At the very last moment, Joel leaned down and scooped Jill up just before she hit the floor directly in front of the couple.

The woman let out a little shriek and raised her hands to protect her baby. When she saw Joel and realized there was no threat, she relaxed and gave a tinkling laugh before grasping her husband's arm.

They resembled a Christmas card; Joel on the last stair with a subdued child in his arms while the couple smiled and introduced themselves. Now that the crisis had been averted Christy was reluctant to join the sophisticated group. But then Jill caught sight of her hovering in the background and her choice was taken away.

Jill sat up in Joel's arms, her lips doing that trembling 'don't be mad, I didn't mean to,' thing she liked to do to get herself out of trouble.

Joel's brows puckered. He looked distinctly uncomfortable with the bundle he was holding. Then he noticed her and the relief was almost comical.

"Christy, there you are." He took the last step and moved to her side, a warning look in his eye. "I was just about to come find you." Ignoring her confused glare, he turned to the couple, his grip firm on the squirming child. "It's getting late and we promised this one she could see the parade. It was nice to meet you, maybe we can talk another time."

Jill held out her arms and Christy moved closer, her fingers brushing corded muscle as she reached for her daughter.

"Imagine, Hank," the friendly young woman said. "We travel halfway across the world for the holidays and run into one of my very favorite authors." Her gaze was filled with curiosity as she looked back and forth between Christy and Joel, but she was too polite to ask about their relationship. Instead she turned limpid brown eyes on Joel and asked for an autograph. "I know you must get a thousand of these a day, but I would be sooo grateful." She rubbed her swollen stomach. "I can't wait to tell junior when he gets older his mommy met the famous Joel Carpenter. I have all your books, you know." She glanced at her husband. "I do, don't I, Hank?"

Hank rearranged his faintly bored expression and smiled his indulgence of his wife's excitement. "Hard to say for sure, that library of yours is overflowing. But now that you mention it, I do believe I've looked at his face on the back of a book you've been reading in bed a time or two, yes dear."

"Oh yes, Augustus is so… well, manly," she said, her cheeks turning a becoming pink. "I've been waiting just forever to read about his next adventure. Is the book coming out soon?"

Joel looked pained, and much as she was enjoying his discomfiture, Christy decided to step in and give him an out.

"The parade is about to start, we'd better go find a spot." She nodded to the couple. "Joel was kind enough to take time out of his busy schedule to join us for the festivities. I know he's been working hard to get the next book done. I had to practically beg him to come." She laughed and transferred Jill to her other arm. "Ready, munchkin?"

Jill lifted her head off Christy's shoulder and gazed at her with drowsy eyes. "I don't feel good, Mommy."

Everything else got pushed aside as Christy's instincts kicked her in the gut. Shoot, with all the excitement of the day, she'd forgotten to do a blood glucose check and give Jill a snack.

She hurried to set her daughter down on the nearest flat surface, which happened to be the stair at Joel's feet, and reached into Jill's go-bag for her monitor and testing supplies.

She forced a smile and held out her hand for one of Jill's fingers. "Let's have a check, shall we?" Her heart stuttered, and she forcibly put a lid on her fear.

Jill leaned on the railing, her face a pale blur against the marble. "I'm dizzy," she whined.

"I know, honey. Hang on, okay?" Christy hurried to take the sample and waited for the machine to tell her what she already knew, Jill was in need of sugar.

Joel dropped beside her and cuddled her tiny frame, his expression grim even as his voice teased. "Hey now, none of that. You don't get to skip the noisy old truck parade that easily."

Warmth flooded Christy's chest as her daughter giggled.

"They're singing trucks, silly. They're supposed to be noisy."

Christy handed Jill some sugar pills and waited while she chewed them down, avoiding the sympathetic stares of onlookers. The couple expecting the baby had faded into the woodwork, not that she could blame them. They were probably worried it was contagious. She'd seen it before. Lived it with her ex-husband.

It didn't matter, none of it mattered as long as Jill was okay.

Joel ran a gentle hand over her child's head as it rested on his arm. Instead of sympathy or aversion, as she expected, his gaze held a compassion that brought a lump to her throat. The urge to curl up on his other side and let him take care of them was overwhelming.

But she knew how that story turned out, and there was no happy ending.

So she bent over the kit and continued to clean up from her hasty dumping of everything earlier, relieved that Jill's color was slowly returning to normal. They would need to retest in fifteen minutes, but already she could see a vast improvement—thank God. She'd never be able to live with herself if her negligence caused any lasting damage.

"You should have told me," Joel murmured, his tone quiet so as not to disturb the resting child.

Christy glanced up, then away. "And what? Beg you to let us stay? No thanks. I'm not that desperate."

He sighed. "You are the most stubborn, ornery, obstinate woman I've ever met."

She couldn't argue with the man. Her pride often caused more problems than it did solutions. But she refused to ever again be a man's charity case—it hurt too much.

CHAPTER THIRTEEN

Joel sat at his desk and frowned at the blinking cursor. Augustus was waiting to rescue the fair Rebecca from the clutches of a nasty landlord holding her at his mercy. Cue the suspense music and evil laughter. The problem was his heroine didn't want to be rescued. She was frustratingly independent and driving him—and Augustus—crazy.

The sky was leaden beyond the sunroom windows, adding to his gloomy mood. How was he going to tie up all the loose ends and come out with a satisfactory ending? He should be working on edits already and he didn't even have the blasted thing written. If only the characters would do as he wanted them to, but they tended to have minds of their own, like a certain strawberry-blonde he knew.

Joel was surprised by how much he'd enjoyed spending the day with Christy and her daughter. Even the unfortunate incident with the girl had done little to ruin the experience of seeing their eyes sparkle brighter than all the lights on the floats. He'd placed Jill on his shoulder for a while so she could see better and had felt about ten feet tall at the resulting warmth of Christy's smile. Gazing at all the other families enjoying the parade his chest had filled with an odd ache.

He wanted what they had.

A wife and child to call his own. The satisfaction he'd known as a successful writer dimmed beside the loneliness of his life. The more time he spent with Christy and her daughter, the more he came to care for them. Jill was a sweetheart, her disability doing little to curb her bubbly personality.

And Christy.

She was so much more than he'd expected. Her tough outer shell hid a woman who would do anything for the people she cared about. She worked tirelessly to do the best she could for her daughter and he respected that. She was the complete antithesis of his own mother, who valued a career more than her child.

Christy was smart, beautiful, and sexy. She'd turned his world upside down and made him a better person for it. All the pent up anger and hostility he hadn't even been aware of disappeared. He felt born again, his emotions as fresh and innocent as a newborn babe's.

He was in love.

Joel sat back and blinked, his chair giving a little creak of annoyance. He'd always pictured love as akin to being hit with a ton of bricks. This was more like landing on a bed of goose down.

Soft.

Serene.

Peaceful.

They could live here. The house was plenty big enough for a family, even if they chose to have more children. Kids. Joel grinned. He couldn't believe he was contemplating asking a woman he barely knew to share his life. But it felt right. Living with Christy wouldn't be easy, she would keep him on his toes each and every day—he pictured her rosy red lips and delectable body pressed close to his—but it would be worth the battle.

Wind lashed rain against the window, startling him out of his daydream.

The phone rang. No one had this number except his agent and Grannie.

He shrugged off his sudden disquiet and hit the speaker button to answer the call. "This better be good, I'm on a deadline."

Grannie's frantic voice crackled over the line. "Joel, come quick. They're leaving."

His blood turned cold. His hands gripped the arms of his chair, fingers white against the dark leather. "What do you mean, leaving?"

For a moment he was that lost little boy again, watching from his second story bedroom as his parents gave last minute instructions to the staff, then turned and followed their suitcases out the door without even a smile for the child left behind.

"I tried to tell her, but she wouldn't wait." Grannie's sobs filled the room. "She thinks she has no choice. Please, Joel, you've got to do something."

What could he do? How could he make her change her mind? He'd already told her she could stay—until she found something better. What an idiot. Of course she would think she still needed to move. She wasn't a mind-reader.

He cursed and pushed out of his seat, his pulse pounding in his ears. "Where was she going, Grannie? Did she say?"

"The ferry, son. She's leaving the island."

He looked at the time. It would be close, but come hell or high water he planned on getting there before it sailed.

"I'm on the way. Keep your fingers crossed for me, Grannie." He grabbed his keys and started for the door.

"Lead with your heart, child. That's all you can do," she murmured.

Indeed. But would it be enough?

CHAPTER FOURTEEN

Christy kept a tight grip on Jill's hand as they wandered the upper deck of the ferry while waiting for departure. High as they were, the breeze still kicked the spray and briny scent of the water up to them. She might have been able to think of this as a grand adventure if they weren't leaving Joel, Claire, and the island.

"Mommy, sailboats," Jill said, tugging her toward the railing.

Whoa, it was a long way down to the water. Christy's vision swam and her stomach went into a spiral. She closed her eyes and inhaled the sea-laden air, then re-opened them with her blurry focus fixed on the horizon.

"How many do you see?" she asked, hoping to keep Jill's attention while she developed her sea legs.

"There's three, seven, eighteen," Jill jabbered, her youthful enthusiasm taking some of the sting out of their departure. Some, but not all.

The car was parked three flights below packed to the gills with their belongings and a moving company had been hired to bring the rest in a couple of weeks—as soon as she figured out where they were going.

Or even where they would be for Christmas.

Claire had begged them to stay. Christy wanted nothing more than to throw caution to the wind and agree, but her feelings for Joel stopped her. She'd done the unthinkable and fallen in love with another man like her ex-husband, someone who placed work above family. She couldn't go through that again. So, yes, they were running. The worst of it was Joel had fooled her into thinking he cared, that maybe he was different and would make time for Jill if they were together. But since the parade he had disappeared. No calls, no sudden appearances, nothing. And she'd known—it was time to leave.

"Mommy, are you paying 'tention?" Jill tugged on her hand.

Christy re-focused on her child, her shiny penny curls tossed by the wind. "Of course, sweetie. I always pay attention to you." She crossed two fingers on her other hand at the fib. "It's chilly out here, we should go inside."

Whitecaps sent sprays of foam high into the air where they splashed against the pier. The overcast sky promised to give them a choppy ride across the strait. She hoped it wasn't an omen. Going back to her hometown already felt like giving up. At the same time, she had her baby to worry about. If that turned out to be her only choice, she'd have to take it. Kevin might not have been a great husband or father, but he'd always been a good provider. He would ensure Jill had the care she needed.

They seemed to be nearly the only idiots left outside. Raindrops splashed their faces as they turned and hurried toward the cabin of the ship. Christy lifted the flap of her jacket and held it over Jill's head as a makeshift umbrella. There was one other guy battling his way through the rising wind to reach the doors.

He arrived moments ahead of them and held the door. Christy glanced up to thank him and froze.

Joel.

She caught her breath, and gasped, "What are…?"

She stared at him, shocked and confused. He'd followed them? Her traitorous heart knew the answer it most wanted to hear, but her more sensible brain told her not to get her foolish hopes up.

He ushered her forward. "Let's talk inside, this weather is crazy." His hand on her back was firm and solid and oh-so reassuringly safe.

The door closed on the wild weather and left them standing in a cozy little nook out of sight of the other passengers. She took a quick step away from the temptation of turning into his chest and holding on tight to brush Jill's wet clothing down and straighten her own before finally facing him.

Jill didn't have the same problem. "You came on the ferry, too, Joel? Are you coming with us to see my daddy?"

Her innocent words sucked the air from the cabin. Joel stiffened, his expression turning as gloomy as the weather beating against the glass behind his head.

"Not this time, honey," he said. "I just wanted to talk to your mom for a minute." He patted his coat pocket, then tugged a high tech cell phone out, and with a few taps, handed it over to Jill. "I saw this the other day and thought you might like it."

"Minions," Jill cried, her eyes lighting up with excitement. "Thanks, Joel."

Christy's throat tightened as she watched them. Her little girl was normally shy, but Joel and his grandmother had become the family they'd dreamed of having. And what about Joel? He liked to play the tough guy, yet he downloaded a silly game he saw because it reminded him of Jill? That wasn't the type of man who thought only of himself and his career. Maybe she'd made a mistake.

"We need to talk." Joel's voice whispered over her nape and a whole host of goose bumps sat up and cheered.

She rubbed her arms and lifted her head defiantly. "I think it's a little late for that, don't you?"

His brows lowered over eyes that were more violet than blue in the dismal light of the foyer. She absently noted the absurd length of his lashes; women paid big money to get that look.

"Weren't you even going to say good-bye?"

He sounded almost hurt, but that was ridiculous. They meant nothing to each other. A couple of close encounters did not constitute a relationship, though the way her heart was pounding it begged to differ.

"I spoke to Claire. I guess she told you." She glanced at Jill to make sure she was safe, then refocused on Joel's shoulder. "Why are you here? We've said everything there is to say."

She sucked in a startled breath when he reached out and tipped her chin so that she had to meet his gaze.

"Did we?" he asked. "Because I have something to say, and this time you're going to listen."

She opened her mouth to speak and he used just enough pressure to seal her lips closed.

"Nope. Me first. You've had this enormous chip on your shoulder since we met." He held up his hand when she frowned. "Okay, I deserved some of it for confiscating your work, but still, you refused to give me a chance.

"As soon as I heard of your struggle I was more than happy to help, and no, it wasn't charity, so get that thought out of your lovely head." He dropped a hard kiss on her mouth, slowing to a questing touch that sent her heart tumbling.

"Give me a chance. I know you've been hurt before, but I'm not that guy." He laid gentle kisses across her puckered brow. "Come home, baby. Come back to where you belong."

Christy closed her eyes and breathed in the very essence of this man she'd grown to care about. He'd followed them. He must have driven like the devil to get to the ferry before they left. It told her he wanted to give whatever was growing between them an honest try.

And as she opened her eyes and stared at his endearing face, she realized she wanted that too.

EPILOGUE

It reminded Christy of a fairy tale. A canopy of twinkling lights above the outdoor skating rink twinkled in the sapphire sky over their heads. The shops circling the courtyard decorated with poinsettias and wreaths in holiday red, green, and gold, added to the festive atmosphere, while giant candy canes led the way to lit paths through the winter gardens. It was a mild evening and required nothing more than a cardigan to be comfortable.

Christy glanced up from tying Jill's skates as Joel returned with fragrant cups of hot chocolate. "This is amazing, Joel. How do they keep the rink frozen with no snow?"

He grinned, his face lit with youthful enthusiasm. "That's part of the magic. Who's ready to give it a try?"

"I am, I am," Jill chanted, wriggling to get down from the tabletop.

Christy hurried to grab her under the armpits, setting her onto her feet and hanging on for balance. "Slow down, missy. We don't want any broken bones before Santa comes."

"Santa's comin' to town 'n' he's keeping a list, so I better be good," Jill sang off-key, mangling the well-known Christmas tune.

Christy thought it had never sounded better. In the two weeks since their return her daughter's blood sugars had stabilized, business was hectic, and they had spent every free moment with Joel. Life was good.

"C'mon, Mommy, it's our turn," Jill said as Joel finished tying his laces, excitement adding sparkle to her hazel eyes.

Joel smiled at her enthusiasm and made a way through the throng, his hand warming the small of Christy's back.

The crowd flowed onto the ice in a sea of caps and tunics amid much laughter and giggles. Christy wobbled for a few seconds, her hands out like a tightrope walker until she regained her stability. By then Joel had Jill halfway across the ice. He was skating backwards and had a firm grip on her hands, helping her to learn how to balance on the narrow blades. Her laughter ringing across the ice lightened Christy's heart. She stopped her awkward momentum and watched the two most important people in her life bond. It had taken awhile, but she had a feeling they were going to be okay.

***

Joel nodded encouragement to Jill and skated slowly backward in a figure eight, allowing her to follow at her own speed. He kept one hand holding on for balance and otherwise let the girl gain some confidence in her abilities. She was doing admirably for being a new skater, and loving every minute of it, if the mile-wide smile and glowing cheeks were anything to go by.

He searched the crowd and finally located Christy along the rails on the far side of the rink. For an Alberta girl she wasn't very sure on the ice. He'd have to work on that in the future.

The future.

He liked the sound of that. These two filled his thoughts and dreams with more love and happiness than he'd ever felt before. He'd even given poor Augustus a happy ending. Instead of the detective saving the girl, the girl saved him. Just like Christy and Jill had done for Joel.

As he steered Jill across the ice toward her mother, Silver Bells played over the speakers, and Joel smiled, for he'd already received his Christmas wish.

A family to Love.

Afterword

In early 2015 our lives changed forever. My then seven-year-old grandson was diagnosed with Type 1 Diabetes.

In the following months we took many classes to learn how to care for his disease. We learned that without proper care and management this is a life-threatening disease.

You can imagine how it felt to hear those words.

With time we've learned to cope, and for the most part he's doing well.

My daughter is the strongest person I know, handling this situation on top of a full university course load. We are so very proud of her.

About The Author

JACQUIE BIGGAR is a bestselling author of Romantic Suspense who loves to write about tough, alpha males who know what they want, that is until they're gob-smacked by heroines who are strong, contemporary women willing to show them what they really need is love. She is the author of the popular Wounded Hearts series and has just started a new series in paranormal suspense, Mended Souls.

She has been blessed with a long, happy marriage and enjoys writing romance novels that end with happily-ever-afters.

Jacquie lives in paradise along the west coast of Canada with her family and loves reading, writing, and flower gardening. She swears she can't function without coffee, preferably at the beach with her sweetheart. :)

Free reads, excerpts, author news, and contests can be found on her web site:

http://jacqbiggar.com

You can follow her on at

http://Facebook.com/jacqbiggar ,

http://Twitter.com/jacqbiggar

Or email her via her web site. Jacquie lives on Vancouver Island with her husband and loves to hear from readers all over the world!

Newsletter- http://eepurl.com/2MFvX

Also By Jacquie Biggar

Wounded Hearts Series

Tidal Falls- Wounded Hearts #1

The Rebel's Redemption- Wounded Hearts #2

Twilight's Encore- Wounded Hearts #3

The Sheriff Meets His Match- Wounded Hearts #4

Summer Lovin'- Wounded Hearts #5

Wounded Hearts- Boxed Set

Coming soon- Maggie's Revenge

Mended Souls Series

The Guardian- Mended Souls #1

Coming soon- The Beast Within

www.ingramcontent.com/pod-product-compliance
Lightning Source LLC
Chambersburg PA
CBHW061253170626
46809CB00007B/2978